All The Mamas

A True Love Story for
Mothers and Daughters
of All Ages

Written and Illustrated by
Carol Gandee Shough

SUMMERHOUSE PRESS
COLUMBIA, SOUTH CAROLINA

Dedicated to my Mama, Catherine,
and
to my Mama-in-law, Thelma

the two best grandmamas
my children could ever have.

Published in Columbia, South Carolina by Summerhouse Press

Copyright 1998 by Carol Gandee Shough

Summerhouse Press
P.O. Box 1492
Columbia, South Carolina 29202
(803) 779-0870
(803) 779-9336 fax

Manufactured by Friesens Corporation, Altona, Man., Canada

FIRST EDITION

Library of Congress Cataloging-in-Publication Data
Shough, Carol Gandee--
     All the mamas : a true love story for mothers and daughters of all ages
  / by Carol Gandee Shough.
          p.   cm.
     Summary: Based on genealogical records from one family, this story
briefly recounts historical events as experienced by generations of
mothers and the daughters they loved and cared for.
     ISBN 1-887714-29-4 (alk. paper)
     [1. Mothers and daughters--fiction.] I. Title.
     PZ7.S55883A1 1998
     [Fic]--dc21   98-14368
                                                        CIP
                                                        AC

10 9 8 7 6 5 4 3 2
The illustrations were created in oil pastel and colored pencil.

This story has no beginning. It has no end.
It's just a slice of time.
We'll start with now and end with then.
We'll start with a girl named Madeleine.

This baby's name is Madeleine.

When she was born, the world was linked by webs and nets.
Computers sent words around the world as fast as
you could blink.

And Madeleine's Mama was wired into this net.
She worked hard as this was faxed and that was saved.
The keyboard clicked, the printer hummed.
While Madeleine slept, the work was done.

When Madeleine awoke, it was time for play. Her Mama
pressed "save" and "quit" and pushed her chair away.
She rushed to see her baby's smile and hear
her laugh out loud.

Her Mama called her Maddie.
"Maddie, Maddie, who loves this baby?
Who loves this pretty baby?"
Her Mama whispers, "I do."
And all the Mamas whispered, "We do, too."
Her Mama laughed with her and played peek-a-boo. She stroked her hair and washed her face and tickled little toes.

And this I know, I know for sure.
Maddie's Mama held her, kissed her, loved her.
Just as I love you.

Now, Maddie's Mama's name is Jenni.

When Jenni was a little girl, the world watched as astronauts in silver suits walked upon the moon. The step for mankind, that magic leap, was seen from there to here. The future seemed quite bright.

And Jenni's Mama nourished sweet promises of future thoughts. She taught. In school by day, at home at night, the family loved and learned.

When the lunar spaceship made its slow descent, Jenni dozed before the TV screen. Jenni's Mama gently stroked the sleepy girl and whispered soft and low:

"J-Bear, J-Bear, wake up, wake up.
We'll watch the landing on the moon."

Her Mama read to her of space, and other fairy tales come true. She helped her with her math. She walked her to the school bus stop and waved as Jenni left.

And this I know, I know for sure.
Jenni's Mama held her, kissed her, loved her.
Just as I love you.

Now, Jenni's Mama's name is Carol.

When Carol was a little girl, the world was waging a terrible, cruel war. All wished to do their noble part and heed their country's call.

So Carol's Mama grew a garden on a wee, small plot of land. She sowed the seeds and watered them. And then she pulled the weeds. When all was ripe she picked the peas, the corn and broccoli, too. With all that work and all that care the Victory Garden grew quite well.

Since Carol was just a wee, small thing, she tottered round the garden plot. She spilled the seeds and broke the strings. But Mama didn't scold. Instead she called her to her side and spoke her special name.

"Squee, Squee, come put some seeds into this hole. Corn and beans will sprout here soon."

10

Her Mama fed her sweet vegetables picked from that
good-smelling earth. She kept her healthy, safe and
sound. She sheltered her from harm.

And this I know, I know for sure.
Carol's Mama held her, kissed her, loved her.
Just as I love you.

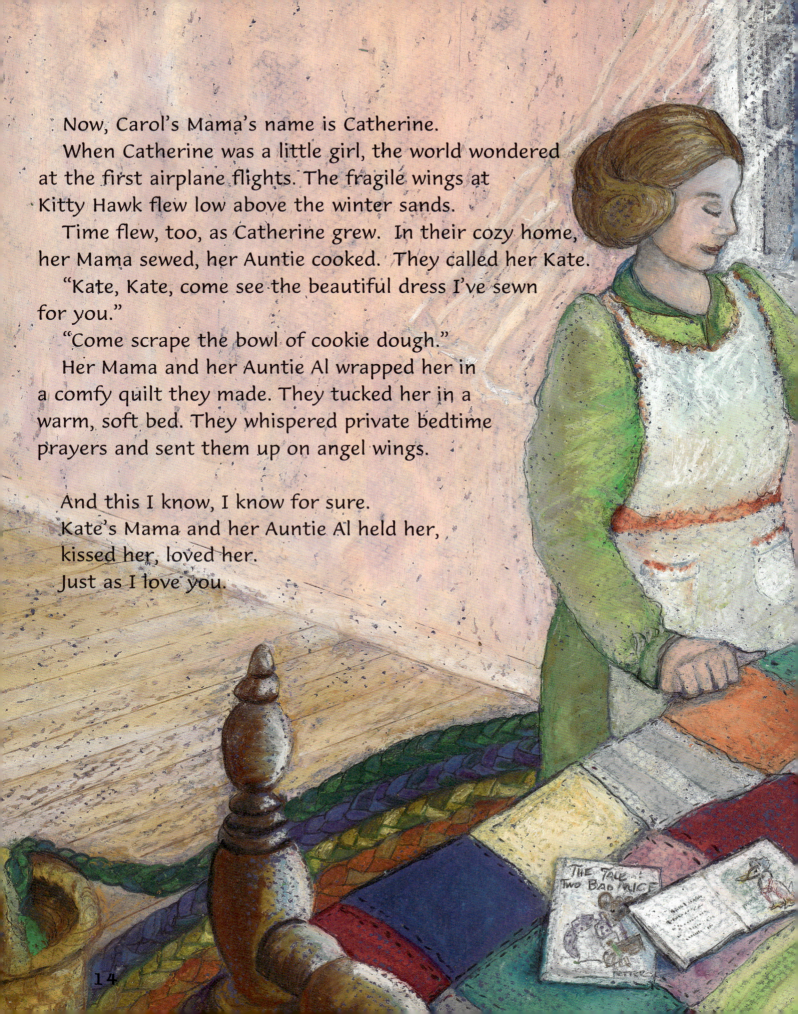

Now, Carol's Mama's name is Catherine.

When Catherine was a little girl, the world wondered at the first airplane flights. The fragile wings at Kitty Hawk flew low above the winter sands.

Time flew, too, as Catherine grew. In their cozy home, her Mama sewed, her Auntie cooked. They called her Kate.

"Kate, Kate, come see the beautiful dress I've sewn for you."

"Come scrape the bowl of cookie dough."

Her Mama and her Auntie Al wrapped her in a comfy quilt they made. They tucked her in a warm, soft bed. They whispered private bedtime prayers and sent them up on angel wings.

And this I know, I know for sure.
Kate's Mama and her Auntie Al held her,
kissed her, loved her.
Just as I love you.

Now, Kate's Mama's name is Mabel.
Her Auntie's name is Alice.
When the two were little girls, the world was changing
rapidly. All thought the wonders of the world were here.
Steam engines moved the speeding trains; machines could
weave the wool. Five older brothers talked about these
things they learned at school.

But Mabel was very little then, the youngest of the
bunch. While her brothers were away at class, her Mama
taught her songs and such. She taught her riddles (some
quite hard) and they were best of all.

When family gathered round at suppertime, the riddles would begin. All the boys tried to answer fast and first, but none could get it right. Then Mama pulled her near to her and whispered in her ear: "Mabel, Mabel, here's the clue." For her Mama made quite sure that only Mabel knew.

But later Mabel grew quite old, and was a child again.
She'd call and call into the night:
  "Mama, Mama, is that you?
  "Come pick me up. Come take me home."
  The night nurse told me so.

And this I know, I know for sure.
  Mabel's Mama held her, kissed her, loved her.
  Just as I love you.

19

Now, Mabel's Mama's name is Carrie.

When Carrie was a young, sweet lass, the States were split in two. Brothers fought and brothers died as others tried to mend the rift. Carrie tended Rebel boys in war camps of the North. She brought them food and washed their wounds. She nursed them back to health.

In years before the Civil War when she was but a babe, her Mama cared for her. She cradled her in tired arms, and nursed 'til Carrie slept. She softly crooned a traveling song while the family westward crept.

"Carrie, Carrie, my little one, we're on the mighty Miss."

Her Mama kept her close and warm while on that drafty riverboat. And as the paddlewheel churned upstream, and charged around the bend, she clutched her baby to her heart and fought the strong north wind. She wrapped her tightly to her chest and soothed her red, chapped skin.

And this I know, I know for sure.
Carrie's Mama held her, kissed her, loved her.
Just as I love you.

Now, Carrie's Mama's name is Mary.

When Mary was a little girl, the world seemed very small. All neighbors, family, and their friends knew each other well. Each knew the farm down by the mill and the store beside the church. Each knew who married whom and when. Each knew when one was hurt.

But Mary's world grew wider still when kith and kin moved on. The wagons filled with family things rolled down the dusty roads. Through dense, dark woods and sunlit glens the wagon train kept on. The travelers reached their new found place and built the family home.

Mary's Mama worked quite hard to make the house a home. She fetched the wood and washed the clothes. She darned those smelly socks! She gathered eggs and plucked the hens. She made a "shoo fly" pie.

"Mary, Mary, come sit with me beside the fire.
We'll spin the yarn and wind the skeins.
We'll save wool scraps and piece the quilt."

Her Mama raised her well. She fed her food and made her clothes. She taught her how to read.

And this I know, I know for sure.
Mary's Mama held her, kissed her, loved her.
Just as I love you.

Now, Mary's Mama's name is Rachel.
When Rachel was a little girl, the word
"liberty" was often heard. When Redcoat
soldiers finally came, she watched her Papa
ride to war.
"Rachel, Rachel, don't you cry."
But Rachel's Mama cried with her.

And this I know, I know for sure.
Rachel's Mama held her, kissed her, loved her.
Just as I love you.

Now, I don't know the name of Rachel's Mama.
    The written words of marriage bonds are forever
lost in time. The vows were said, but none now know
the when and where of it.

    And this I know, I know for sure.
    Her Mama held her, kissed her, loved her.
    Just as I love you.

The names of all the Mamas past are now forgotten whispers in the wind.

For sure one Mama crossed the wide waters of the sea.

For sure one Mama worked within cold, castle walls.

For sure one Mama walked through fields of wheat.

For sure one Mama washed clothwraps of wool.

For sure one Mama wove slender reeds and willow twigs.

For sure one Mama whistled low beside a glacier cliff.

For sure one Mama whittled tools of bone.

For sure one Mama watched through treetop heights the hunt down on the plains.

For sure all Mamas rocked their young.
They held them, kissed them, loved them.
Just as I love you.

J
SHO

Shough, Carol Gandee

All the mamas

$16.95

DATE			